DANITRA BROWN
LEAVES TOWN

DANITRA BROWN
LEAVES TOWN

written by
Nikki Grimes

illustrated by
Floyd Cooper

HarperCollinsPublishers

Amistad

Amistad is an imprint of HarperCollins Publishers Inc.
Danitra Brown Leaves Town
www.harperchildrens.com

Library of Congress Cataloging-in-Publication Data
Grimes, Nikki.
  Danitra Brown leaves town / by Nikki Grimes ; illustrated by Floyd Cooper.
      p.   cm.
  Summary: Recounts, in a series of poems and letters, Danitra's summer at her aunt's house in the country and her best friend Zuri's summer at home in town.
  ISBN 0-688-13155-7 — ISBN 0-688-13156-5 (lib. bdg.) — ISBN 0-06-075311-0 (pbk.)
  [1. Summer—Fiction. 2. Best friends—Fiction. 3. Friendship—Fiction. 4. City and town life—Fiction. 5. Country life—Fiction. 6. Afro-Americans—Fiction.
7. Poetry—Fiction. 8. Letters—Fiction.] I. Cooper, Floyd, ill. II. Title.
PZ7.G88429 Dan 2002
[E]—dc21   00-069725
                                                                                                                 CIP
                                                                                                                 AC

Typography by Matt Adamec   ❖

For Mike and Claudette McLinn
and Melanie Donovan,
Danitra's godparents
—N. G.

For the Flournoy family
—F. C.

Big Plans

School is out soon
and Danitra's advice is:
surrender
to
summer,
to
raspberry ices
and
pink lemonade
and
walks on the beach
and
at least
one
trip to the zoo,
one
Ferris wheel ride,
one
family barbecue,
one
Sunday school picnic,
but
never a lick
of
homework to spoil
one
afternoon.

The Bad Good-bye

Danitra talked a blue streak
about her summer trip
all week.
And now that she is on her way,
she has the nerve to call and say
which station she is leaving from,
as though expecting me to come.
"I have better things to do," I blurt.
The phone is silent. Danitra's hurt.
But why am I supposed to care
when my supposed-to-be best friend
is leaving me, and loving it?

Noticing Nina

Summer insisted on starting
for no good reason that I could see.
I was alone, with nowhere particular to be.

One day Nina from the neighborhood
said she wondered if we could
play a little handball. I'm famous for the game,
but I never knew that Nina liked it too.

She and I spent hours slamming that ball
against the corner drugstore wall
wearing a hole in the bricks.

Later, we talked and laughed awhile,
and after we said good-bye, I wondered why
I'd never noticed Nina before.
Maybe the summer wouldn't be such a bore.

The Letter

I sat frowning by my window
when the mail truck came today
with a letter from Danitra
who is many miles away.

I said mean things when she left me.
I was so mad at her then.
Was she writing to forgive me,
or to say I'm not her friend?

I ripped Danitra's letter open,
in spite of my worst fear.
I bit my lip until I read
"I wish that you were here."

First Night

Dear Zuri,

I wish that you were here.
I camped out my first night
in my aunt's backyard.
Sleeping was hard
with all the sparkling beauty
hanging overhead.

Night-lights, Zuri, everywhere!
Clusters of fireflies
dancing 'round my head,
keeping me from bed
for hours.

And the sky! I've never seen one
so blue-black, like a thick overcoat
all buttoned up with stars.
At midnight, I stretched my arms out
to slip the darkness on,
and opened my eyes again
at dawn.

Block Party

Dear Danitra,

Tomorrow you're going to miss
those giant speakers
hissing and blasting
loud, fast music
into the crowded street.
There'll be no sense in my
trying to keep still.
You know how
that hot, hot dance beat
sizzles up through the concrete,
grabbing hold of my feet.
In a blink I become
a hip-swinging,
head-bobbing,
foot-stomping,
fancy-dancing
fool.

The Dare

Dear Zuri,

The kids here pretend to be tougher than they are.
I ignore it mostly, 'cause they're nice in their own way.
Besides, I think they may just be trying to impress the "city kid."

Today they dared me to climb up into a tree, and, of course, I did.
Then they yelled, "Okay, Miss Big-Town Brown, jump down."
Now, my mother taught me to use my head for more than a hat rack.

So, I climbed back down and said, "A dare is fine with me,
but jumping from a tree is stupid, and I'm no fool."
Then I heard someone whisper, "She's pretty cool—
for a city girl."

Zuri at Bat

Dear Danitra,

At the softball game last week,
smart-mouth J. T. snickered loud and said,
"What makes you think a puny girl like you can help us win?"
"Exactly where *you* been?" I asked him, stepping in.
When the pitch came, I slammed the ball so far,
it ripped through the clouds and headed for a star.
I strutted 'round the bases, took my own sweet time.
My new friend, Nina, laughed and bet J. T.
he couldn't hit a ball as far as me.
He can't, and that's a fact.

A Different Danitra

Dear Zuri,

You'd probably laugh
if you saw me now.
I'm not exactly behind a plow,
but still—here I am, in the dirt
on hands and knees,
yanking weeds,
watering roses,
dodging man-eating wasps
and one stubborn dragonfly,
who I'm convinced
wants me for lunch.
I have a hunch
you'd like it here.
There's a lake near,
and tomorrow I thought
I might go
skinny-dipping!

Zuri's Fourth of July

We had the day
all to ourselves,
to search for seashells
on the beach.
To eat corn dogs
and candied apples.
To stroll awhile and talk
and skip along the boardwalk—
just Mom and me.
Seeing my mom skip
was worth the stuffy subway trip
it took to get there.

The holiday
seemed barely
long enough
to measure,
but I loved spending the day
with my mom next to me,
the pretty brownness
of her eyes and face
glistening in the light
of the late-night
fireworks.

Danitra's Family Reunion

On the Fourth of July,
my cousins and I
ran sack races,
played kickball
and tug-of-war
before
we heard
our stomachs
growl.

We stopped for
deviled eggs,
buttered corn,
coleslaw,
fried chicken,
potato salad, and
Strawberry Pie Jubilee.

We sipped lemonade
and listened to
Grandma Brown's stories
of when our folks were little.
Then Uncle Joe
handed out prizes
for this year's graduates
and for the best all-round student,
which I won.

By the time
the day was done,
I was full of fun
and food
and warm feelings,
knowing that I am more
than just me.
I am part
of a family.

Dream Places

Dear Danitra,

Since you left,
I've put a map on my bedroom wall.
I stick gold stars on all the places
I'll travel to someday:
Zaire, Hong Kong, Bombay.
I find each city in my geography book,
look up the facts and figures,
and write them down in the diary
I keep beside my bed. I lay my head
back on the pillow, close my eyes,
and see myself, a little older,
walking down an African street,
soaking in the heat of the sun.

Home Again

A good hello
is knowing
when we're far apart,
at heart
we're still together,
and being glad
you're home again
'cause that is ten times better.

Nikki Grimes

calls writing her first love and poetry her greatest pleasure. Her ever-popular books include MY MAN BLUE; JAZMIN'S NOTEBOOK; the Coretta Scott King Honor Book MEET DANITRA BROWN, illustrated by Floyd Cooper; and IS IT FAR TO ZANZIBAR?, illustrated by Betsy Lewin. Ms. Grimes has conducted readings and lectures at colleges and universities across the country, as well as in Europe and Africa. She lives in Corona, California.

Floyd Cooper

is the acclaimed illustrator of many children's books, including A CHILD IS BORN by Margaret Wise Brown, I HAVE HEARD OF A LAND by Joyce Carol Thomas, and AFRICAN BEGINNINGS and BOUND FOR AMERICA by James Haskins. Mr. Cooper received a Coretta Scott King Illustrator Honor for BROWN HONEY IN BROOMWHEAT TEA in 1994 and again for MEET DANITRA BROWN in 1995. He lives in West Orange, New Jersey, with his wife and two children.